In the Playhouse

by Anne Giulieri

illustrated by Omar Aranda

My cat
is in the playhouse.

My dog
is in the playhouse.

My bird
is in the playhouse.

My rabbit
is in the playhouse.

My fish
is in the playhouse.

My mum
is in the playhouse.

13

My dad
is in the playhouse.

15

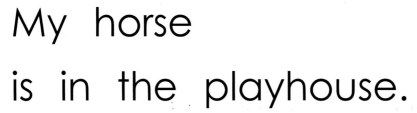

My horse
is in the playhouse.

16